POOF...AND THEN IT VANISHED

VAISHNAV KARTHIKEYA

Made with ❤ on the Notion Press Platform
www.notionpress.com

To my Mom, Dad, Grandma and Grandpa

Also To my good friend Siddha Smaran

Contents

FOREWORD

"Loved it... amazing story" -Mom

"I was mesmerized after reading...really loved it" -Siddha

"Nice Story"-My Aunt

"Always knew you were good at making stories" -My Mamaya

Preface

This is just a small story that started off as an English Assignment

The Party

With warm lights covering the sky, and food and drinks everywhere, peoples laughs filling my ears, people ever so dear to me. A place I called home and with people I called my family, I cheerfully blew out the candles when the clock struck 12. The cake was huge with a big 16 on top, it was all perfectly fine till it happened.

The day was my birthday when I was surrounded by happiness, and then within a blink of an eye, it all vanished. My happiness, family and my ever-so-beautiful home, took nothing but a split second for me to be alone. It was all so sudden, I didn't realise what had happened at first. Just moments ago I was surrounded by everyone I knew and loved, and when I blew out those candles it all became blank. "What has happened to everything, and everyone around me", I thought. It was as if everything disappeared into thin air. When last I was so happy but in pain. A sharp pain in my chest when I blew out those candles on top of my sweet 16 cake, and then it all vanished with the ever-so-painful sting in my chest.

The Realisation

Soon, I realised that it was I who vanished, but what worried me more was the thought of not returning. Not returning to my family and my perfect life, with the slightest of problems. I will surely miss my wonderful friends, my beautiful house, and the people who make it home for me. All the planning for my career gone to waste. Worrying over worthless things, when at last all that mattered were the good times.

THE END...

Thank you all... hope you've enjoyed my short and simple story. Will surely make many more improvements and hopefully will publish another one soon!

9 798888 499641